Dance with Rosie

For my dear grandmothers:
Anna, who wished to be Anne,
and
Jennie, who wished to be Genevieve,
with love

Dance with Rosie

by Patricia Reilly Giff

illustrated by Julie Durrell

VIKING

Thank you to Doris Driver, Director of the New England
Academy of Dance in New Canaan, Connecticut

VIKING
Published by the Penguin Group
Penguin Books USA Inc., 375 Hudson Street, New York, New York 10014, U.S.A.
Penguin Books Ltd, 27 Wrights Lane, London W8 5TZ, England
Penguin Books Australia Ltd, Ringwood, Victoria, Australia
Penguin Books Canada Ltd, 10 Alcorn Avenue, Toronto, Ontario, Canada M4V 3B2
Penguin Books (N.Z.) Ltd, 182-190 Wairau Road, Auckland 10, New Zealand

Penguin Books Ltd, Registered Offices: Harmondsworth, Middlesex, England

First published in 1996 by Viking, a division of Penguin Books USA Inc.

1 3 5 7 9 10 8 6 4 2

Text copyright © Patricia Reilly Giff, 1996
Illustrations copyright © Penguin Books USA Inc., 1996
All rights reserved

LIBRARY OF CONGRESS CATALOGING-IN-PUBLICATION DATA
Giff, Patricia Reilly.
Dance with Rosie / by Patricia Reilly Giff; illustrated by Julie Durrell.
p. cm. — (Ballet slippers ; 1)
Summary : Rosie tries to make up with her former best friend and get into ballet class
after the sign-up deadline.
ISBN 0-670-86864-7
[1. Ballet—Fiction. 2. Friendship—Fiction.]
I. Durrell, Julie, ill. II. Title. III. Series: Giff, Patricia Reilly. Ballet slippers ; 1.
PZ7.G3626Dan 1996 [Fic]—dc20 96-14695 CIP AC

Printed in U.S.A.
Set in OptiBrite

Chapter 1

It was Saturday, before breakfast. I sneaked a quick look out the window.

Not sneaky enough.

Amy Stetson spotted me in two seconds and waved. She was doing butterflies on her porch. Ballet butterflies. Warm-ups, she called them.

That's all Amy did. She practiced ballet a thousand hours a day.

That reminded me. There was something I

had to find out about right this minute, before I had one bite of breakfast.

I raced out the door, and headed for Scranton Avenue. I had to see that sign, the one Karen Cooper had told me about.

On the way, I passed Tommy Murphy, my old best friend. He was racing up and down on his lawn, making motorcycle sounds. "I see you, Rosie O'Meara," he said. "Spying on me."

He would never have said that before our fight two weeks ago. Now we weren't best friends anymore. We weren't even friends. I wanted to say, "How come, Murphy?"

Instead, I just kept going. I didn't stop until I saw the pointed roof of the Crow's Nest Country Store.

And there in the window, in large letters on a pink sheet, was what I was looking for:

BALLET
SEVEN-TO-TEN-YEAR-OLDS

DANCE WITH MISS DEIRDRE!
SIGN UP ON THE TENTH OF JUNE

I sat down on the curb. I had always wanted to be a ballerina. I could see myself flying across the stage, people clapping, a hundred tutus in my closet, like Amy.

Miss Deirdre was going to change my life.

I stretched out my legs, and looked at my long skinny feet. Mouse feet, my grandfather called them. I closed my eyes. In my mind, I rounded out my feet. I could see pearly pink nail polish on my toenails.

My legs became ballerina legs.

I stood up slowly, gracefully, like a ballerina. I could see myself wearing a white net tutu, and a tiara that sparkled.

I started back along Scranton Avenue, dancing on my toes.

I could hear footsteps behind me.

Murphy.

"Now who's spying?" I yelled.

But I knew he wasn't spying. He was going to get the paper for his mother.

I twirled once, twice, and started a third twirl.

It made me dizzy . . . too dizzy to see Mrs. Maxwell's garbage cans until I was almost on top of them.

I tried to stop short, but I could tell it wouldn't work. Instead I jumped . . . jumped as high as I could, and just cleared the garbage cans.

I landed on the other side. On my knees. I'd have sores on them for a month. I opened my mouth to cry.

But in back of me, someone was clapping. "A *grand jeté*," the someone said. "A great leap."

I looked around.

A lady was sitting on the steps of the Crow's Nest Country Store. She had frizzy red hair, and freckles almost as big as mine. Her leg had

a black-and-blue mark as big as a tennis ball.

I snapped my mouth shut and tried to act as if my sore knees belonged to someone else.

Then there was another voice. Murphy's voice. "Great leap," he said, "for a frog."

I ducked my head and took four ballerina steps away from Murphy and the lady. Then I twirled around the corner and back toward home . . . home for breakfast, and a cool washcloth for my knees.

Chapter 2

Grandpa was sitting at the table waiting for breakfast. His stuff was piled around him on the table: his newspaper that was folded to the crossword puzzle, a dictionary, and two pencils sharpened to absolute points.

"Rosaleen O'Meara," he said, "I see you've skinned your knees again."

I had forgotten all about them, but now they started to hurt again.

"It was terrible," I said. "The most enormous…"

Grandpa looked up. His blue eyes were twinkling. "Car?" he asked. "Truck?"

"Well..."

"Animal?"

"Yes. I had to dive into the bushes to escape." I slid into my seat, keeping my knees stiff.

"That's another lie, Rosie," my little brother, Andrew, said from under the table.

Grandpa winked at me. He flipped through his dictionary. "I have something for you. A magazine picture. I put it in here so it wouldn't wrinkle."

I looked at it. A dancer, on her toes, looking a little like Amy Stetson. "I'll take it," I said.

My father was rushing around with breakfast: those doormat cereal things for Grandpa, and eggs for Andrew and me.

"This egg could have been a bird," I said.

"A hen," said Grandpa. "Not the same thing at all."

"Don't be silly, Rosie." My father sat down

12

with the rest of the apple pie. It was a fat piece, left over from the other night. "Don't tell Mother," he said, and looked up at the ceiling.

We could hear my mother clicking around upstairs. She was getting ready for work. She sold pictures in an art gallery all day—pictures of deer with antlers, and mountains with snow on their points.

Andrew, under the table, was drawing a picture for her to take with her. It looked like a black-and-white box.

He held it out. "A cow," he told us. "Mother will love it."

"I love it, too," I said, smiling at him. I tried to see which end was which.

I poked a fork in the top of my egg. "No good," I said. "Juicy."

"Two bites, please," my father said.

"Have a doormat," Grandpa said.

I closed my eyes and took a little of the egg white. I grabbed a banana with speckles. Then

I went up to my room with the ballet picture and a roll of Scotch tape.

Almost no space was left on the walls. I walked around looking at my pictures. One ballerina was dressed as a white swan. Another was Sleeping Beauty. On the side of my dresser was Cinderella, a dancer holding a glass slipper.

I slapped the new ballerina up on the other side. Gorgeous. Someday I was going to be all of them.

Outside, I could hear Murphy's lawn-mower sounds. And something else, too.

It was Karen, the new girl, talking to that poor nerd, Robert Ray.

Karen was lucky. She had long hair, not chopped off for the summer by Albert the barber.

She was calling me. "Ro-zzzzeeee."

One thing about Karen I loved. She had the loudest mouth in Lynfield.

I waved to her. Then I sank down under the

windowsill. There was something I had to think about. A worrying something. I'd been feeling it since I had seen the lady at the Crow's Nest Country Store this morning.

It had to do with the picture. Not the one on the side of the dresser—the one over my bed in the gold curlicue frame.

I looked up at the picture of Genevieve, the ballerina. Genevieve, my grandmother.

She had feathers covering her hair. Her toes were pointed, and one leg was stretched up high. Grandpa said she was doing a *grand battement.*

She was absolutely beautiful. Grandpa thought anyone would be lucky to be just like her, and that my dark hair was the same color as hers. It was a good start, I guess.

If only I could be a ballet star like Genevieve … or like thirteen-year-old Amy next door.

I looked out the window. Amy was on the porch again, her hair up in a gorgeous brown bun. She was sitting on the porch floor, the soles of her feet together and her knees out. She was moving her knees up and down slowly like wings. Butterflies again.

They were hard to do.

I'd never be like Amy or my grandmother Genevieve. I was probably going to turn out like that frizzy freckled lady with the black-and-blue mark.

And another thing. The thing about Murphy. How was Murphy ever going to be my best friend again, if I didn't even know what was wrong?

Chapter 3

It turned out that the frizzy lady's name was Miss Serena and she was the piano player.

It turned out that Miss Deirdre was the ballerina, and lessons would start on Monday. I found all that out from Mr. Mooney at the Crow's Nest Country Store on Saturday afternoon.

"That's good," I told Mr. Mooney. "Absolutely good. I'm going to sign myself right up."

I bought three gigantic gum balls instead of two, just because I felt this syrup of happiness.

The syrup of happiness ... that's what Mrs. Hamilton, my teacher, always says she feels when everything is going better than she thought it would.

And because Mr. Mooney was doing nothing but running a dishcloth over the counter, I had to ask him if he wanted to share a gum ball.

He shook his head *no* so I stuck two in my mouth, and slipped the other one in my pocket.

"See you," I told him.

I started down the street, looking back at the store. A nest really was jammed up under the pointed roof.

Murphy had seen it first. It was large and messy, and he had promised me, absolutely, that it was a real crow's nest ... even though Mr. Mooney had said there hadn't been a crow around for years.

I passed my house, and waved at Grandpa.

He was up on a ladder, painting. He was taking long, slow swipes with the brush. Grandpa never hurried.

But Andrew was in a hurry. He dipped a stick into the can, dripping dots of white all over the place. Paint was on his face, his hair, his sneakers. When Grandpa looked down, he'd have a fit.

But I wasn't a tattletale. I went next door to Amy's. I needed some ballet pointers, to start me out ahead of everyone else.

I wanted to be the star at Dance with Miss Deirdre.

I couldn't see Amy through her porch window, so I started along the side of her house. I stopped when I saw Murphy skateboarding up the street.

I waved, kind of an almost-wave, in case he didn't wave back.

He didn't.

I could hear Grandpa shouting, "Andrew!

What are you doing to my paint?"

I grinned, and leaned my head against Amy's screen door. Mrs. Stetson was putting her plants on the kitchen table. "Here's Rosie," she told a stringy-looking plant. "Amy's upstairs."

I went up to Amy's bedroom. Amy has the best bedroom in the world. Net tutus were tossed over a chair. Ballet slippers, pink, and black, and white, were piled underneath.

I leaned over to pick up one of the slippers. It was soft in my hands. I could see the shape of Amy's toes. I ran my finger around the edge.

I'd have slippers of my own. Pink and soft like this one.

"I'm going to take lessons," I said to Amy's back. "How about—"

"How about you sit with me and I'll show you a thing or two," she said from the floor.

"How about I try one of the tutus to see what it feels like?" I asked.

"Don't take the white one," she said. "You'll have it filthy in one minute."

I ran my hands over my shirt. Amy was right. They were a little sticky from the gum balls.

I looked down at the tutus. It was hard to make up my mind: the black tutu with sequins, or the red one with gold strings dangling all over the place?

I grabbed the black, and stuck a diamond tiara on my head.

"Take your sneakers off," Amy said, sniffing a little. "You have gum on them, too."

She was right again. I pulled them off with the backs of my feet. Then I settled myself down next to her, stretching my legs forward.

"We'll do flexes," she told me. "Keep your legs flat on the floor, and point your toes to the ceiling."

"Easy," I said.

"Now, pull your toes closer to your legs.

'Hello, toes.' And then down toward the floor. 'Goodbye, toes.'"

"Easy," I said again.

The trouble was we waved our toes back and forth forever, with Amy telling me that ballet was ninety-five percent strength. "Got to make those babies tough," she said, pointing to our waving feet.

"My toes are ready to say good night," I told her.

I stood up and slid out of the tutu and into my sneakers. "Can I wear the tiara for a while?"

"If you get that into a mess—" Amy began, still wiggling her toes.

"I won't," I called back, racing down the stairs, holding the tiara on with one hand. No wonder Amy went to the city for lessons four days a week. If they spent all that time on toes...

I headed for Karen's house. I thought about taking a shortcut through the alley behind the stores on Scranton Avenue. But I didn't. We were still in big trouble with Mrs. Delano, the candy-store lady. Murphy and me.

We had been running through the alley, capturing creatures from outer space. Mrs. Delano had come out the back door of Delano's Delicious Chocolates, and we had gotten her instead of an alien.

We had stomped on her foot. Twice. Me first, and then Murphy.

She was probably still wearing a bandage.

I took the long way around, and found Karen in her garage. Every inch was covered with horse pictures: horses jumping over fences, horses eating hay, horses hanging around in fields.

Karen waved her hand around, "I was going to take all of this down, but now…" She leaned forward. "Neat tiara." She raised one shoulder. "I wanted to get ballerina pictures like yours, but now that we can't take lessons, I don't know…"

I picked up her cat, Toby, listening to the sound of his purring. "You aren't going to take lessons?" I was all set to say it wouldn't be any fun without her.

She looked sad. "We can't."

"What are you talking about?" Toby's sharp little claws were digging into me.

"We were supposed to sign up this morning," she said.

I shook my head *no* and reached into my pocket to hand her a gum ball. "It was the tenth," I said.

Karen popped it into her mouth.

A mistake. I should have waited. It took forever for her to talk around the gum.

"Today's the tenth," she said. "I don't know how we forgot."

I didn't say anything for a minute. I knew she was right. I was always doing stuff like that, mixing things up. I swallowed.

"Don't feel bad," Karen said. "Maybe we can

take horse lessons or something this summer."

My jaw hurt from chewing the gum for so long. Everything hurt. The syrup of happiness was all gone.

"I think I have to go home," I told Karen. I put the cat down on an old rug. "Andrew's in the paint, and my grandfather needs me."

I was glad Karen didn't tell me to stay. I had just enough time to get out of there, down the stairs, and out the door, with the tiara falling over my eyes, before I began to cry.

Chapter 4

Karen was right. Everyone had signed up ahead of us. My mother called on Sunday, and that's what they told her.

Grandpa even walked me over to the store on Scranton Avenue. I kept my head down as we went by Delano's Delicious Chocolates.

DANCE WITH MISS DEIRDRE was written on the brand-new awning in blue letters.

Grandpa and I could have stayed home. A sign was pasted on the window:

SORRY. THE CLASSES ARE FILLED.

Grandpa rapped on the door with his knuckles. "Terrible business," he said. "I was all set to buy you ballet slippers, and—"

A woman popped her head out of Gee-Gee's Toys next door. "You want to break the window?"

He gave the window another sharp *rat-tat-tat*, then stopped. "Come on," he told me.

We walked up Scranton Avenue. I could see ourselves in the store windows. Grandpa was tall and a little bent. I looked ready to cry.

Grandpa began our game. "When I saw the sky..." he said.

"Everything had disappeared?" I asked.

"Well, something was glowing..."

We both sighed. We were too sad to figure out what came next.

"You're telling lies, Rosie," Grandpa said in an Andrew voice.

I tried to smile, but my mouth wouldn't move.

Grandpa cleared his throat. "Well. You'll have more time to do things with Tommy Murphy."

I didn't answer.

"Murphy—" Grandpa began again.

"Murphy's not my best friend anymore. He's not even my friend," I said. "We had a fight. I don't even know about what exactly."

Grandpa sighed again. "Never mind about the ballet. If you want it enough, it'll happen someday. You'll make it happen."

"That's what Mrs. Hamilton, my teacher, always says," I told him.

"Mrs. Hamilton sounds neat." He smiled.

And that's when, suddenly, I had the best idea of my life.

When I told Karen, she said, "This is why you're always in trouble." But I knew she was going to do it with me.

"We'll have to wear dark clothes," I said.

"Why?"

I shook my head. One thing about Karen, you had to explain everything. Murphy would have known what I meant in two seconds.

"Just wear something dark," I said. "Then no one will see us. Put your leotard on underneath."

"I don't have—"

I closed my eyes. "Wear anything then."

Karen was making kind of a little mouth, chewing on her lips. She did that whenever she was annoyed, so I smiled.

She smiled back.

"I'll meet you right after school. *Right after,*" I said, to make sure she wouldn't be late.

And that's how we found ourselves in the alley behind Dance with Miss Deirdre on Monday afternoon. We tiptoed past Gee-Gee's Toys and Hot Bagels and Delano's Delicious Chocolates.

I was wearing my mother's black sweater. It came down to my knees. I kept my chin under

31

the top button like a turtle. No one would know me in a million years.

Karen was wearing red sweats.

The alleyway was an absolute crowded junk heap. There were garbage cans from Hot Bagels, puddles of water, a barrel, and a kid's old blue jacket lying on the ground.

Karen was making a mouth again.

"Don't worry," I told her. "I'll make a great space for us."

I moved the garbage and pushed the cans out of the way. I tossed the blue jacket over the barrel. "See," I told her. "Easy."

Karen was looking up and down the street.

"You're worried about those kidnappers," I said.

Karen nearly jumped out of her skin.

I had forgotten. Karen wasn't Murphy. She wasn't Grandpa.

"I'm just kidding," I said.

She kept looking back over her shoulder. I

yanked the blue jacket off the barrel, and spread it out. "Sit here," I said.

"It would be just my luck—" she began.

"To meet up with a kidnapper?" I tried not to laugh. All we had to do was screech. Everyone in Lynfield would be on top of us in a second.

I knelt on one end of the jacket and peered in the back window of Dance with Miss Deirdre.

Miss Deirdre wasn't so good about cleaning windows.

I rubbed at the window with the blue jacket, until I could see the room clearly.

On one wall was a mirror. In front of it was a wooden bar. *Barre,* it was spelled. I knew that from Grandpa.

A pile of kids were sitting on the floor, and—I caught my breath. I could see Miss Deirdre. She was wearing black tights with pink leg warmers. Her hair was pulled back in a bun with a velvet ribbon.

Gorgeous. She wouldn't go to Albert the barber in a million years.

Miss Serena was there, too, swaying back and forth at the piano, thumping out up-and-down sounds.

"Joy of movement," said Miss Deirdre. "Beauty of line." She waved her arm. "First we practice at the barre, holding on. Look in the mirror. Make sure you look graceful."

She clapped her hands. "Warm-ups, every-one."

This was it, I thought. Butterflies or Hello, Toes.

But it wasn't either one. It was turtles with long necks. "Raise your heads up high out of your shells," Miss Deirdre said.

Pam de pam pam, played Miss Serena.

"...and look to the right, then the left. *Grace-ful-ly.*"

"Let me see, will you, Rosie?" Karen whispered, but I was pulling off my mother's sweater.

I was wearing a white leotard underneath. Grandpa had given it to me last month for getting three math hundreds. I was wearing Genevieve's heart necklace, too. I wore it on special occasions only.

Karen was pushing. I pushed back.

After all, the whole learning-how-to-dance-in-the-alley business had been my idea. Miss Deirdre was talking about first position now. It was one thing to miss turtles with necks, but if I didn't see first position, how was I ever...

"Shoulders open," said Miss Deirdre. "Soft hands, knees straight."

"Just give me a look," Karen was saying. And before I could even stand up to get my knees straight, she pushed again.

I banged into the window hard enough for Mrs. Delano to hear me four stores down.

Everything stopped.

Miss Serena raised her hands above the piano.

Kids pointed up at us.

I didn't stop. I grabbed the jacket, flew over the garbage cans again, and raced for home, with Karen right behind me.

Chapter 5

I was out of breath when I reached my front path, the blue jacket trailing off in back of me.

I hadn't even noticed that Karen had peeled off on Nancy Place to get to her house.

No one was following me.

But someone was yelling.

It was Murphy on his bicycle.

"Thief!" he was shouting. "Stealer!"

"You're crazy!" I yelled back.

"I think your front light's out." He crashed his bike into his front steps on purpose.

He thought he was so tough.

I marched up the front path and into my bedroom. I sank down on the floor, my turtle neck high out of my shell, saying hello to my toes.

I had paint from Andrew on my shoes.

"Andrew," I shouted. "Your front light's out."

He came to my bedroom door. "What does that mean?" he asked. "My front light's out?"

"Never mind," I said. "Could you just get out of here, and let me be by myself?"

"You're in trouble again."

"I am not." I wondered what I had done with my mother's sweater. Left it there, left it in that dirty alleyway, and now I was stuck with a ratty old blue jacket. I shoved it under the bed and waited for Andrew to go somewhere else.

When he did, I closed my door tight.

I looked up at Genevieve doing her *grand battement*. I wished she had lived to be old like Grandpa.

One time Grandpa had told me she would have taught me ballet, and the steps for the *Nutcracker* and *Swan Lake*, and how to lace my slippers.

He had started to say something else, but his lip was trembling. I knew he was close to crying.

Quickly I'd started our game. "I think robbers are in the garage," I said. "They're stealing your fishnet and all your hooks."

Grandpa had smiled a watery smile. "Ten of them. Don't worry," he said. "I'll capture them after supper."

But right now, looking up at Genevieve, I remembered what Mrs. Hamilton and Grandpa had told me: If you want something enough, you'll make it happen.

I looked out the window, across to Amy's bedroom. She was using her dresser for a barre, and walking one foot up the side of her leg. I could see her lips moving.

I knew what she was saying, even if I couldn't hear her. *Hickory dickory dock. The mouse ran up the clock.* I had heard her do that a thousand times.

If that's what I had to do—Turtles, and Hello Toes, and Mice—I'd do it.

Amy turned, and saw me looking at her. I waved, and she waved back, pointing to her head.

I put my hand up to my mouth. I had forgotten to bring back her tiara. I had left it on the hall table. "Sorry," I mouthed.

I looked up at the picture. "Don't worry, Genevieve," I said. "I'll learn ballet if it kills me. And when I do, I'll never go to Albert the barber again. I'll have my hair long in a bun, and there won't be any scabs on my knees either."

I stood next to my bed practicing first position: hands soft, shoulders open, and knees straight.

Then I sneaked over to the window to see

what Murphy was doing. He was just sitting there, next to his crashed-up bike, doing nothing.

I wanted to call, "Hey, Murphy, turn on your front light." But I didn't even know what it meant.

Chapter 6

It was the next lesson day that I remembered Amy's tiara. It looked a little bent, so I had to wiggle it back and forth. I hoped she wouldn't notice.

I wanted her to show me second and third positions up close before I got to Miss Deirdre's window. A little head start. I'd been practicing from a library book all weekend, and I kept getting mixed up.

Amy was on the phone when I got there.

She took a quick look at the tiara and frowned.

I thought about waiting, but I was late . . . and who knew what she'd say when she got off the phone anyway?

I hurried to the alley, saying the positions by heart. Second: elbows up, feet not too far apart, hands soft. Third: one arm up over your head, the other arm out, feet touching. At the same time, you were supposed to put the heel of the right foot in the middle of the left. Whew!

Karen had gotten to the window first. She was hogging the whole thing.

Inside, everyone was hanging on to the barre with one hand for balance. All I had to hang on to was Karen's shoulder.

And she kept twitching me off. "How can I put my arm over my head with you in the way?" she asked. She stuck out her other arm and poked me in the eye.

She certainly wasn't graceful.

But neither was I. I kept falling into the

wall. If only I had ballet slippers, pink and soft, instead of last winter's sneakers.

I could see a girl over Karen's shoulder. Her tongue was sticking out the corner of her mouth as she did the positions. She looked like Murphy's dog, Homer.

The lesson was over by five o'clock, and I was home again.

"Did you find my sweater, Rosie?" my mother asked.

I put my hand up to my mouth. It was still bunched up against the windowsill in back of Dance with Miss Deirdre.

"Maybe you left it at the Crow's Nest," my mother said. "Why don't you take a run down?"

I stood up. Absolutely perfect. I'd make a quick stop at the Crow's Nest Country Store. Then I'd head over to Miss Deirdre's. I'd grab the sweater, and—I could feel the syrup of happiness—I'd try the back door of the dance studio. I'd see what it felt like to be inside.

And that's what I did. I checked the crow's nest, but nothing was happening. No babies, no parents.

Mr. Mooney treated me to a gum ball. "Pick a color," he said.

I rooted around until I found the biggest red one. I held it with two fingers and made a pale line around the middle with my tongue.

"I haven't seen Tommy Murphy lately." Mr. Mooney's head was turned to one side. He was looking at me from under his eyebrows.

I waved my hand toward the street. "Murphy's around somewhere."

The truth was, outside of the school yard, I hadn't seen him all week.

"You two used to be thick as thieves," Mr. Mooney said. He sounded like Grandpa.

"What does that mean?" I asked, but Mrs. Delano had come in for red pepper, and I dashed out.

I stopped at the corner to do a long turtle neck, then the first, second, and third positions. When I figured no one was looking, I ducked into the alley, head down. I was a turtle disappearing into my shell.

Murphy was in Gee-Gee's. I could see one of his ears through a hole in the window display. I'd know Murphy's ears anywhere. He hated them, but I thought they were great. They were big, and flat, and the tops almost stuck to his head.

The day we stopped talking, I remembered, his ears were red. So were his face and his neck. Red as Santa's coat, Grandpa would say.

And I didn't know what it was about . . . something to do with the crows and the nest at Mr. Mooney's store. I stood there thinking about it. Then I heard someone opening the door to Delano's Delicious Chocolates.

I ducked past quickly. I stood behind a garbage can until the door was shut again.

My mother's sweater was still on the windowsill. I scooped it up and dusted it off. It didn't dust very well. My mother was going to have a fit.

I twisted it around my neck so I wouldn't forget it. I peeked in the back window. It was shiny clean on the outside from the spraying I had given it yesterday.

It was almost dark inside, and empty.

If the door wasn't locked...

And it wasn't.

I tiptoed down the three steps, turned the handle to the inside door. I was in.

I yanked off my sneakers and felt the smooth wood of the floor with my feet, and the barre with my hands.

I didn't look in the mirror. I didn't want to see Albert's chopped-off haircut, or my freckles and brown scabbed knees.

I turtled and flexed. I did the positions I knew. Then I was Genevieve doing a *grand bat-*

tement. I was Genevieve doing a *plié*, a *tendue*, a *relevé*... things Grandpa had told me about.

Of course, I didn't know how. But I'd learn.

I could feel the syrup of happiness in my chest, honey-colored, sweet, and smooth.

Then I started over, holding on to the barre. First position, second, third.

"And fourth," someone said. "Elbow back over your head. Then make the other elbow round, and turn out your feet."

I did as she said, hardly able to breathe, my heart banging in my throat.

I looked into the mirror.

It was Miss Serena, frizzy and freckled, doing the positions for me, and then a *grand battement*, just the way Genevieve was in the picture.

Chapter 7

"*Betsy Beneath*," my grandfather said, leaning back in his chair.

My mother was smiling at him.

I sat back, too. I absolutely loved this story.

"Now that is where Genevieve came from," said Grandpa. "It was called that because Betsy, an old thief, was buried *beneath* one corner of the town."

Andrew looked up. His mouth was filled with pasta. "When did that happen?" he asked.

"Don't worry. It was a million years ago," Grandpa said. He laughed.

"Where?"

"In Betsy Beneath," I said, laughing, too.

"That's a lie, Rosie," Andrew said.

"And Jenny," said Grandpa, "was always afraid when she walked past—"

"So she danced past," I said, watching Andrew, waiting for him to tell me it was another lie.

I would have been so happy sitting there, ready to tell them I was going to have ballet lessons after all. I wasn't even going to worry about telling where my mother's sweater had been.

But Murphy popped into my head. Murphy's nice flat ears. And his neck with a speck of dirt on it.

On the way home, we had crashed into each other. The scab on one of my knees had opened up, and there was a sharp pain in my side from

Murphy's elbow. After supper, I'd tell Grandpa I might have a broken rib.

Murphy leaned over. He was rubbing his shin, trying to catch his breath. He stood up when he saw me watching. He was too tough to let me see he was hurt.

"The best thing just happened," I told him, forgetting for a moment we weren't friends.

He leaned forward. I thought he was smiling.

"I'm going to take ballet lessons after all," I told him. I was so glad to be talking to him. I couldn't stop smiling. "Both of us. Me and Karen. I can't wait to tell her."

I guess I imagined that he was listening, that he was smiling, too.

He bent his head to look at his leg. He was frowning. I could see a tiny spot of blood on his jeans.

"Feels terrible?" I asked, full of sympathy.

He put his nose up close to mine. "You stole my jacket," he said.

"Your front light is out," I said. I didn't have one speck of sympathy left. I didn't have a drop of the syrup of happiness, either.

Murphy made his eyes into slits. "Your brain took a walk and forgot your head," he told me—

"I think she's not listening," someone else said.

It was Andrew, at the dinner table. He was drawing a great big cow again. He was using drops from the pasta sauce to make red spots all over the cow.

And Grandpa was still talking about Betsy Beneath. "We went over there to see Genevieve's father," he said. "She *tendued* and *relevéd* over his cabbages and red radishes."

"And she was beautiful," I said.

"Of course," Grandpa said.

I sat there chewing on Mr. Mooney's red radishes. I thought about Genevieve, and my chance to take ballet lessons, and frizzy Miss

56

Serena doing a *grand battement.*

I watched my mother smiling at Grandpa, and my father nodding, and Andrew slurping up a piece of ziti.

And then I thought of Grandpa and Mrs. Hamilton. If you wanted something hard enough, you'd get it, sooner or later.

And what I wanted, most of all, was to be Tommy Murphy's best friend again. Somehow, I was going to make it all work out.

I just didn't know how.

Chapter 8

There was no time to think about Murphy now.

It was the first day of my real ballet lessons.

I waited forever for Karen to get her stuff together. Then we made a mad dash over to Scranton Avenue. We ducked under the awning that said DANCE WITH MISS DEIRDRE, and went in the front door.

Kids were all over the place, getting ready.

I *was* ready. Grandpa had taken me down to Alden Bootery for the most beautiful ballet slippers I had ever seen. They were pink and so soft you could bend them. Then Grandpa had hung my grandmother's pointe slippers over my bed.

I couldn't wait to tell Miss Deirdre about my grandmother.

I danced up to the barre...gracefully...and picked a spot in the middle. I'd be able to see everything, and Miss Deirdre would see me. I had practiced every single minute of my spare time.

A moment later, Karen slid in on one side of me, and before I knew it, some kid who was missing a front tooth tried to elbow her way in between us. It was the kid whose tongue hung out like Murphy's dog, Homer.

"I'm here," the kid said, in a fresh voice, as if you could save yourself a spot on the barre.

"Your front light is out," I told her, holding

on to the barre with both hands.

It was just my luck that the kid was a major tattletale. Miss Deirdre waved at me with one gorgeous pointy finger. I ended up at the absolute end of the line.

I caught Karen's eye in the mirror, and waved at her. I tried to keep my finger as pointy as Miss Deirdre's.

It seemed fair that Karen would march herself down next to me.

She didn't. She was lifting her foot up as high as she could, trying for a *grand battement*. She had seen Genevieve's picture fifty times.

I raised my hand.

Miss Deirdre nodded at me.

"My grandmother was a ballerina," I said. "Her name was Genevieve—"

Before I could get the rest of it out, Miss Deirdre nodded again. "Lovely." She clapped her hands. "First position, girls."

"... famous," I said a little louder, but everyone was making their hands soft and their knees straight.

I sighed and made my knees straight, too. My hands were so soft they looked as if they were going to fall off my arms.

I knew what was coming next. I slid into second position, and third. I was just a touch ahead of everyone else, watching Miss Deirdre.

But Miss Deirdre didn't look as happy as I thought she would. "Slow down a little," she told me as she went by. "Put your tongue back in your mouth."

I was sticking out my tongue, too? Like that kid who looked like Homer? I snapped my mouth closed.

"Nicely done," Miss Deirdre told Karen.

Everything went wrong from then on. I watched Karen and the toothless kid whispering to each other, and mixed up third position with fourth. I did a quick hop to get it right.

A noisy hop.

Everyone looked down the row at me in the mirror.

I kept smiling. I made believe I was way ahead of everyone else instead of miles behind. I made up a couple of steps behind Miss Deirdre's back. Everyone would think I had learned a special step from my famous ballerina grandmother, Genevieve.

I was worn out by the time it was all over. We had done the positions a hundred times... and I had mixed them up about ninety-nine.

We practiced *tendues* next, over and over, and Miss Deirdre gave us a paper to take home. It showed a girl doing *tendues:* arms and legs all doing something different.

And then at last it was time to go home. I waited for Karen at the door. Everyone streamed out in front of me.

I heard the toothless girl—Stephanie, I think her name was—ask Karen to come over to her house and practice with her.

I didn't wait to hear what Karen said back.

I banged out the door, rushed down the alley, and headed for the Crow's Nest Country Store.

Chapter 9

How could I go home? Grandpa would be waiting at the kitchen table. He'd look up the minute I came in. "You were the best," he'd say.

And I knew I was the worst.

Karen was calling. I didn't look back.

I dashed around the corner, head down. I crashed into Mrs. Delano.

"Not again," she said, when we had both caught our breath.

I looked down. A fat tan cloth was still

wrapped around her foot. I gulped. "How is your..."

Mrs. Delano looked down, too. "It's coming along, I guess."

"I meant to..." I began, and then I stopped.

"Good girl," she said. "I thought you were going to say you meant to come to the store to find out."

Mrs. Delano was a mind reader.

"I should have said I was sorry," I told her.

Mrs. Delano nodded slowly, and blinked.

She had eyes like a crow. Large and dark. I wished I could tell Murphy that. He'd love it.

"And where is Tommy Murphy these days?" Mrs. Delano asked.

"He's around," I said. I could see a red mark on her other foot.

I didn't know which was worse, to step on the same foot twice, or one and one.

I could see Mrs. Delano smile for the the first time. Usually she was grumpy, telling everyone in the store to hurry up.

I wondered if I was going to cry.

Mrs. Delano really was a mind reader. She handed me a paper tissue. A purple one.

I wouldn't have guessed Mrs. Delano would have colored tissues. I would have guessed white. Plain white.

But then I thought about Miss Serena. She hadn't turned out the way I thought she would, either.

By this time, Karen had caught up. She bobbed her head up and down at Mrs. Delano.

"Whew," she said. "Aren't you tired?"

Mrs. Delano stood there another second. She looked like her old grumpy self again. Then she went off down the street.

I kept my head down. I didn't want Karen to see my red eyes and the purple tissue. She'd know just what I was crying about.

She didn't, though. She held out fifty cents. "I owe you a gum ball. Want to…"

I swallowed.

"Besides," she said. "Wasn't there a nest or something you wanted to show me?"

"A crow's—" I began to say, and bit my lip.

"You always do that," Karen said.

I shook my head. "What?"

"You always begin to say something, and then you stop."

I took a quick swipe across my eyes with the purple tissue. "Allergies, I guess," I said. "Lots of grass floating around. Just like my mother."

"What are you talking about?" Karen asked.

I smiled at her. "Sorry," I said.

"What about the gum ball?" she asked.

I shook my head. "I have to go home."

I couldn't say what I was really thinking.

It was about the fight I had with Murphy that was really over nothing. But somehow it had something to do with the crow's nest.

I just didn't know what.

Chapter 10

Grandpa was on the back steps with Andrew. I knew he was waiting for me.

Andrew was a mess of paint.

"Don't touch a single thing, Andrew," Grandpa said. The whole time he was looking at me.

"I was terrible," I said.

"That's a lie, Rosie," Andrew said. "You're a very nice girl."

"Oh, Andrew," I said, beginning to cry

again. "That's the nicest thing you ever told me."

"Don't cry," Andrew said. "I'll draw you a very good cow."

My eyes filled with tears. I rushed up to my room and picked up my ballet slippers. I held them, patting them the way I patted Jake, our cat, when he was afraid of thunder.

And then Grandpa was there. He sat down on the chair next to the door. It was a small chair from when I was in kindergarten ... too small for him.

"Well." He looked out the window. "I was thinking of Genevieve this afternoon."

I looked out the window, too. Murphy was on his front path, throwing a ball for Homer to catch.

I wished it was last month. I wished it was the day Murphy had found the crow's nest. I wished Murphy and I were best friends again.

I wished the ballet had worked out.

The whole time I was wishing, Grandpa was rocking in the little chair. "About Genevieve." He reached into his wallet.

I sat on the edge of the bed, still watching Murphy, while Grandpa fished through a pile of odds and ends.

Murphy was sitting on the grass, looking at something. It was probably an anthill. Murphy loved stuff like that. Last month, he would have showed it to me.

"Here," said Grandpa. He put a square paper on the bed next to me. It was an old picture, black-and-white, and creased. It was a picture of...

"Jenny," Grandpa said.

I looked closer. It was a little girl with pale hair. She was standing in a vegetable garden, holding something, maybe a bunch of radishes with their green leaves still on.

Grandpa was smiling at me. "Eight years old."

"She looks like Andrew," I said.

"Maybe." Grandpa looked up at the picture over my bed. "She doesn't look like Genevieve."

I shook my head. "No."

"But she is," said Grandpa. "It just took her a long time to get from one picture to the other."

He slipped the picture back into his pocket. "You can't tell much by looking at a picture."

"What does that actually mean?" I asked.

"It means it took a long time for Jenny to become a dancer—for her to become Genevieve," he said. "It means that all we know about people are little bits of things. And it means we have to use our heads to figure out the rest."

"But…" I began.

But Grandpa was on his way downstairs.

I took another look at Murphy, the toughest kid in Lynfield.

And I thought about Murphy who wouldn't kill a worm or an ant. Murphy who had found the nest, and showed it to me because I was his best friend.

And I thought about our fight, the fight I couldn't figure out.

Of course.

All I did was talk about Karen, my new friend. And Murphy must have thought he wasn't my best friend anymore.

And I remembered something else. I had said, "I'll show the nest to Karen."

My mother was calling me for supper.

I went downstairs slowly. Grandpa was right again. I had used my head.

And I had figured it all out.

Chapter 11

Andrew had left a picture at my place at the table.

"It's not a cow after all," he said.

"No, I can see that." I looked at the fat pink blob on the paper.

"It's you," he said, "being a ballet dancer. See your ballet slippers on the bottom? You can put it up in your room."

"I'd love to," I told him. "I'll look at it while I practice."

"Lovely," said my mother, patting me on the shoulder.

I slid into my seat and raced through the tuna salad, and the lettuce and tomatoes. I even took one bite of egg before I put my plate into the sink.

"I just have to get something from my room," I said. "And my ballet slippers for luck. Then I'm going over to Murphy's."

"About time," said Grandpa.

I crossed the street, waving back at Amy on her porch. Murphy wasn't in front, so I went into his yard, my ballet slippers tucked in my pocket.

Murphy was kneeling on the grass, fooling around with some pieces of wire.

"Hey, Murph." I held out the old blue jacket. "I didn't remember it was yours."

He didn't look at me. He just kept twisting the wires.

"I guess you dropped it that day we knocked

Mrs. Delano over." I put it on the step.

Murphy raised one shoulder in the air.

I sank down on the grass and looked at the wires.

"What are you making?" I waited a minute. When he didn't answer, I took a breath. "I never showed Karen the crow's nest," I said. "She's a nice girl, but…"

Murphy wasn't looking at me, but he wasn't twisting the wires.

"She would have said they were sparrows," I said. "Or…"

"Robins," Murphy said.

"Something like that," I said, laughing a little. We looked at each other.

"I say they're crows," I told him, crossing my fingers.

"That's another lie, Rosie," Murphy said in an Andrew voice.

I picked up one of the wires and began to make a circle with it. I wanted to tell him he was my best friend, but he liked to act tough.

I said it anyway. I whispered it, in case he didn't want to hear it. "Murphy," I said. "You're my best friend."

He grinned at me. "Yeah." He tossed the wires down on the lawn. "Want to go over and take a quick look at the nest?"

I nodded, patting my slippers through the cloth of my jacket. "That's what I was thinking."

We started for Scranton Avenue. When I got home I'd practice positions. I'd practice *tendues,* and maybe try a *grand battement.*

Right now, I was Rosie.

But someday, I was going to be Rosaleen, a ballerina.

From Rosie's Notebook

Barre (say "BAR") It's a handrail in front of a mirror. Hold on and warm up!

Battement tendu ("baht-MA ton-DUE") Heel up, slide one foot out, then back. Pretend you have a penny under your toes and you want to keep it there.

Grand battement ("GRON baht-MA") A great kick. I haven't learned this yet, but Genevieve does it in the picture. One leg is thrown up in the air. It looks super!

Grand jeté ("GRON sheh-TAY") A leap! One leg is stretched forward, and one leg is back. This one looks great too.

Plié ("PLEE-ay") Bend your knees out, with your back straight. Look in the mirror. See the diamond shape you've made with your legs. Straighten your knees again.

Relevé ("reh-le-VAY") Rise to the balls of your feet. Keep your toes on the floor. Press down hard. (It's tiptoes.)

First position Put your heels together and turn your feet and legs out to the side. Do your feet make a straight line? (Mine don't yet.)

Second position Move your turned out feet apart about the length of a ruler.

Third position Put one heel against the middle of your other foot. They're still turned out.

Fourth position Put your right foot about ten inches in front of your left foot. They're still turned out. Keep your heels in a line.